W9-CAL-386

The Boxcar Children Mysteries

THE BOXCAR CHILDREN
SURPRISE ISLAND
THE YELLOW HOUSE MYSTERY
MYSTERY RANCH
MIKE'S MYSTERY
BLUE BAY MYSTERY
THE WOODSHED MYSTERY
THE LIGHTHOUSE MYSTERY
MOUNTAIN TOP MYSTERY
SCHOOLHOUSE MYSTERY
CABOOSE MYSTERY
HOUSEBOAT MYSTERY
SNOWBOUND MYSTERY
TREE HOUSE MYSTERY
BICYCLE MYSTERY
MYSTERY IN THE SAND
MYSTERY BEHIND THE WALL
BUS STATION MYSTERY
BENNY UNCOVERS A MYSTERY
THE HAUNTED CABIN MYSTERY
THE DESERTED LIBRARY MYSTERY
THE ANIMAL SHELTER MYSTERY
THE OLD MOTEL MYSTERY
THE MYSTERY OF THE HIDDEN PAINTING
THE AMUSEMENT PARK MYSTERY
THE MYSTERY OF THE MIXED-UP ZOO
THE CAMP-OUT MYSTERY
THE MYSTERY GIRL
THE MYSTERY CRUISE
THE DISAPPEARING FRIEND MYSTERY
THE MYSTERY OF THE SINGING GHOST
MYSTERY IN THE SNOW
THE PIZZA MYSTERY
THE MYSTERY HORSE
THE MYSTERY AT THE DOG SHOW
THE CASTLE MYSTERY
THE MYSTERY OF THE LOST VILLAGE
THE MYSTERY ON THE ICE
THE MYSTERY OF THE PURPLE POOL
THE GHOST SHIP MYSTERY
THE MYSTERY IN WASHINGTON, DC
THE CANOE TRIP MYSTERY
THE MYSTERY OF THE HIDDEN BEACH
THE MYSTERY OF THE MISSING CAT
THE MYSTERY AT SNOWFLAKE INN
THE MYSTERY ON STAGE
THE DINOSAUR MYSTERY
THE MYSTERY OF THE STOLEN MUSIC
THE MYSTERY AT THE BALL PARK
THE CHOCOLATE SUNDAE MYSTERY
THE MYSTERY OF THE HOT AIR BALLOON
THE MYSTERY BOOKSTORE
THE PILGRIM VILLAGE MYSTERY
THE MYSTERY OF THE STOLEN BOXCAR
THE MYSTERY IN THE CAVE
THE MYSTERY ON THE TRAIN
THE MYSTERY AT THE FAIR

The Mystery of the Lost Mine
The Guide Dog Mystery
The Hurricane Mystery
The Pet Shop Mystery
The Mystery of the Secret Message
The Firehouse Mystery
The Mystery in San Francisco
The Niagara Falls Mystery
The Mystery at the Alamo
The Outer Space Mystery
The Soccer Mystery
The Mystery in the Old Attic
The Growling Bear Mystery
The Mystery of the Lake Monster
The Mystery at Peacock Hall
The Windy City Mystery
The Black Pearl Mystery
The Cereal Box Mystery
The Panther Mystery
The Mystery of the Queen's Jewels
The Stolen Sword Mystery
The Basketball Mystery
The Movie Star Mystery
The Mystery of the Pirate's Map
The Ghost Town Mystery
The Mystery of the Black Raven
The Mystery in the Mall
The Mystery in New York
The Gymnastics Mystery
The Poison Frog Mystery
The Mystery of the Empty Safe
The Home Run Mystery
The Great Bicycle Race Mystery
The Mystery of the Wild Ponies
The Mystery in the Computer Game
The Mystery at the Crooked House
The Hockey Mystery
The Mystery of the Midnight Dog
The Mystery of the Screech Owl
The Summer Camp Mystery
The Copycat Mystery
The Haunted Clock Tower Mystery
The Mystery of the Tiger's Eye
The Disappearing Staircase Mystery
The Mystery on Blizzard Mountain
The Mystery of the Spider's Clue
The Candy Factory Mystery
The Mystery of the Mummy's Curse
The Mystery of the Star Ruby
The Stuffed Bear Mystery
The Mystery of Alligator Swamp
The Mystery at Skeleton Point
The Tattletale Mystery
The Comic Book Mystery
The Great Shark Mystery
The Ice Cream Mystery
The Midnight Mystery
The Mystery in the Fortune Cookie
The Black Widow Spider Mystery

THE BLACK WIDOW SPIDER MYSTERY

created by
GERTRUDE CHANDLER WARNER

Illustrated by Hodges Soileau

ALBERT WHITMAN & Company
Chicago, Illinois

Activities by Rebecca Gomez
Activity illustrations by Alfred Giuliani

No part of this publication may be reproduced, or stored in a retrieval system, or transmitted in any form or by any means, electronic, mechanical, photocopying, recording, or otherwise, without written permission of the publisher. For information regarding permission, write to Albert Whitman & Company.

ISBN 978-0-8075-5544-6

Copyright © 2003 by Albert Whitman & Company. All rights reserved. BOXCAR CHILDREN is a registered trademark of Albert Whitman & Company.

10 9 8 7 6 5 4 LB 15 14 13 12 11 10

Printed in the U.S.A.

Contents

CHAPTER 1

New Neighbors

"Look! There goes another truck!" cried six-year-old Benny Alden, looking out the window. "The new neighbors must be moving in!"

"It's about time," his ten-year-old sister, Violet, said. "It seems like the builders have been working on that house *forever*."

"Are you still watching what's going on down the street?" asked their grandfather, looking up from the deck of cards he was shuffling. Grandfather and Violet were playing Go Fish.

"I've seen two moving trucks go by this morning," said Benny. "I think the neighbors are finally coming!"

Henry, who was fourteen, joined Benny at the window and looked outside. "Too bad they put up that big stone wall. I can barely see the top of the house!"

"Why would anyone want a wall that big?" twelve-year-old Jessie asked.

"Maybe they have a whole lot of dogs!" Benny guessed. "I hope so."

Benny leaned closer to the window. As he stood watching the street for more moving trucks, he suddenly saw something else.

A limousine was moving slowly down the Aldens' street. Benny watched as the long, black car with dark-tinted windows turned into the driveway of the new house and disappeared out of sight behind the stone wall. "The neighbors are here!" Benny shouted, jumping up and down. "I just saw them!"

"Really? What do they look like?" asked Violet.

"Well, I didn't really *see* them," said

Benny. "But I saw their car pulling into the driveway. It was a limousine!"

"Wow!" said Jessie. "But you didn't see who was in it?"

"No, the windows were dark — I couldn't see inside," Benny said, disappointed.

"A limousine with tinted windows and a big stone wall," said Henry. "These people sound different from our other neighbors."

"Some people like their privacy," said Mr. Alden.

"That's more than just privacy," said Jessie. "It's almost like they're *hiding*."

Grandfather smiled. "Well, I'm sure you four will do your best to make them feel welcome in the neighborhood."

"We'll go over later and say hello," Henry suggested.

"Let's ask Mrs. MacGregor if we can make a cake to take them," Violet added.

"Good idea!" said Benny, who always got excited about food. "A chocolate cake!" He ran into the kitchen where Mrs. Mac-

Gregor, the housekeeper, was washing the dishes from lunch.

"Mrs. MacGregor!" said Benny. "Will you help us make a cake for our new neighbors?"

"A cake is a lovely idea," Mrs. MacGregor agreed. "Let me just finish straightening up, then we'll make one."

The children had loved Mrs. MacGregor — and her cooking — ever since they'd come to live with their grandfather when their parents died. At first the children were afraid Mr. Alden would be mean, so they had hidden from him. They found a boxcar in the woods and made it their home. But when they learned what a kind man their grandfather really was, they came to live in his large house. He'd even brought the boxcar to their backyard so they could play in it.

Benny helped Mrs. MacGregor finish cleaning and putting away the lunch dishes. She got out the mixing bowl. She and Benny mixed flour, sugar, and baking soda. They added oil and eggs and chocolate.

Soon the cake was in the oven, and a wonderful chocolaty smell filled the house.

"I can't wait to eat it!" Benny said to his sister Violet, who had just come into the kitchen.

"I thought the cake was for the neighbors," Violet said.

The smile on Benny's face disappeared. "That's right," he said sadly. "I forgot."

Mrs. MacGregor laughed. "Not to worry, Benny," she said. "I made some extra batter." Mrs. MacGregor put a tray of cupcakes in the oven beside the cake pan. "These you can eat."

"Hooray!" said Benny, giving Mrs. MacGregor a big hug. "You're the best."

Later that afternoon, Grandfather and the children walked over to welcome their new neighbors. Benny was proudly carrying the cake, which he and Mrs. MacGregor had iced with thick, fudgy frosting.

"No, Watch," Jessie told the dog as they set out. "You have to stay here."

The Aldens crossed the street and walked

down the sidewalk toward the new neighbors' house. "Wow!" said Jessie as they got closer. "The stone wall is even taller than Grandfather! And look at that weird gate!"

A black wrought iron gate stood slightly open at the end of the driveway. The gate was decorated with unusual designs. The Aldens paused to look at the gate more closely.

"It looks like . . ." Henry began.

"Spiders!" said Benny, his eyes wide.

Jessie shuddered. "Why would anyone want giant spiders on their front gate? That's not very welcoming."

"It is rather unusual," Mr. Alden said.

Violet took a step closer, examining the way the wrought iron bars on the gate twisted gracefully into the shape of spiders and intricate webs. "It's pretty cool how they did this," she pointed out. "It's actually kind of beautiful."

"Beautiful?" said Jessie. "I think it's creepy."

Henry pushed the heavy gate further open. He stood still for a moment, looking

up at the house. It was large and imposing, with arched windows and a tall peaked roof. Something about the house looked almost unfriendly.

Slowly the Aldens began to make their way up the driveway.

Benny studied the house ahead of them. He had watched it being built from the ground up. Why did it make him feel so uncomfortable now? He had the strangest feeling that someone inside was watching them.

Benny searched the windows but saw no one. He was glad Grandfather had come with them.

At the front door, Jessie reached for the doorbell but suddenly jumped backward. "Oh my!" she cried.

"What is it?" Henry asked.

"Look at that giant spiderweb!" Jessie pointed over the doorbell.

"And look at the size of that spider crawling in it!" said Violet.

"You're not usually scared of spiders," Henry said.

"I know," said Jessie. "I think I'm just a little nervous after that weird gate and — "

Suddenly the front door began to move. It slowly creaked open, revealing a dark hallway and a tall woman standing inside. She had pale, white skin and long, dark hair. She was dressed entirely in black.

The woman studied Mr. Alden and the children for a long moment without saying a word. At last, in a cold, flat voice she said, "Hello."

"But I didn't even ring the bell!" Jessie said, confused. "How did you know we were here?"

The woman raised an eyebrow. "I saw you coming."

Mr. Alden put out his hand. "James Alden, nice to meet you," he said. "Welcome to the neighborhood. We live right down the street. These are my grandchildren, Henry, Benny, Jessie, and Violet."

"And I am Arachnia Blackwell," said the woman, shaking Mr. Alden's hand. She smiled slightly, but her manner remained cool.

Jessie motioned for Benny to give her the cake. But Benny just stood there, staring. Jessie gently urged him forward with her hand on his back. Benny took a timid step toward Mrs. Blackwell and held out the cake. "This is for you," he said in a quiet voice.

Mrs. Blackwell looked down at Benny. "Thank you," she said, taking the plate from him. Benny immediately noticed her long, red fingernails. They looked sharp and dangerous.

Mrs. Blackwell stepped farther back into the house. "Won't you come in?"

"Why yes, thank you," Mr. Alden said, leading the way. "Benny's been watching the construction here — this house took a long time to build."

"The house was built specially for us," Mrs. Blackwell said. "To suit our . . . unusual needs."

"Unusual needs?" repeated Jessie.

"My husband and I have jobs that are rather . . ." Mrs. Blackwell paused, as if looking for the right word. "Unique."

"What does *unique* mean?" asked Benny.

Mrs. Blackwell smiled. "It means our jobs are different from most people's." She looked around for a place to put the cake. There was no furniture in the hallway, just stacks of boxes. "Oh, what am I going to do with all this stuff?" she said under her breath.

"You sure do have a lot of boxes," Benny said.

Mrs. Blackwell nodded, her face grim. "Yes, we do. I don't know how I'm going to get them all unpacked *and* get my work done."

"We could help you," Henry offered.

"What do you mean?" asked Mrs. Blackwell.

"We'd be happy to come over and help you unpack," Henry said. "We're good at cleaning and organizing. Especially Jessie." He smiled at his sister.

Mrs. Blackwell thought about this for a moment, a slight frown on her face. "I'm not sure my husband would want children touching his . . . things," she said.

"My grandchildren are very careful," said Mr. Alden.

"We've helped out lots of places, even at the Greenfield Museum, and they had some very valuable things," Jessie said.

Mrs. Blackwell suddenly looked quite interested. "Did you say you'd helped at the museum?"

"Yes," Henry said proudly.

"The problem is that some of my husband's things are a bit fragile." Mrs. Blackwell looked around at all the boxes. "Still, it would be nice to have some help." She looked back at the children, studying them thoughtfully. "All right," she said at last. "Why don't you come first thing tomorrow morning and we'll get started."

"OK," said Henry. "We'll see you then."

"Nice meeting you," Mr. Alden said, as he led the children out the door.

As they walked down the driveway, Jessie turned to the others. "There's something unusual about Mrs. Blackwell."

"Yes," Violet agreed. "She chooses her

words very carefully — it's almost as if she's hiding something."

Benny's face lit up. "A secret?" He smiled broadly. "I love secrets. I'm going to figure out what it is!"

CHAPTER 2

A Strange Symbol

The next morning, the Aldens ate a quick breakfast and then walked up the street to the Blackwells' house. They felt excited and a little nervous, wondering what it would be like inside. They had only seen the front hallway and were curious what the rest of the house was like. And would they get to meet Mr. Blackwell?

As the Aldens approached the Blackwells' front gate, a long, black limousine passed them and headed up the driveway. The car disappeared behind the house, so the children couldn't see who was getting out.

When they reached the door, Mrs. Blackwell once again opened it before they rang the bell.

"You're here," she said. She smiled briefly.

"Good morning," Henry said. "Where should we start?"

Mrs. Blackwell looked around her at the stacks of boxes. Some boxes had been partially unpacked. Here and there on the floor were piles of books, pots and pans, and crumpled newspaper. "You can start right here, I suppose. These boxes all need to be carried to the rooms where they belong. I'll give you a quick tour of the house, and then you can take all the boxes where they need to go — they're all labeled on top."

"Sounds easy enough," said Henry.

Mrs. Blackwell's voice suddenly became tense. "When you see boxes with this symbol on them," she pointed to a box that had a red marking on the top, "be extra careful with them. I'll show you where they go. But whatever you do, *don't* open those boxes."

Mrs. Blackwell looked closely at each of the children to make sure they were paying attention.

The Aldens nodded seriously.

"Come along, then," Mrs. Blackwell said, her voice more relaxed. She began the tour of the house.

"This is the living room, the dining room is over there, and here's the library," Mrs. Blackwell said. The Aldens walked quickly, trying to keep up with her. The rooms were dark, lit only by the little bit of light that came in the windows. The Aldens weren't sure whether the Blackwells hadn't unpacked their lamps yet or whether they just liked the dim light.

At the back of the house was a long, dark hallway. At the far end of the hall, the children could see a closed door, with a line of light gleaming from underneath.

"Here's where the boxes with the red markings go," Mrs. Blackwell said. "You don't need to go down the hallway. Just leave the boxes here and my husband will take care of them."

"Are you sure?" Henry said. "We don't mind — "

"Yes, I'm sure," Mrs. Blackwell interrupted. "You are not to go down there or you will disturb my husband. And remember, the boxes stay closed."

Upstairs, Mrs. Blackwell showed them the master bedroom, an office, a couple of guest rooms, and a sitting room. Each room already held several stacks of boxes.

"What does that door lead to?" Jessie asked, pointing to a door off the sitting room.

"That door?" Mrs. Blackwell said. "Oh, that's my — " She suddenly stopped, as if she'd changed her mind about what she was going to say. "Don't worry about that. There won't be any boxes for that room. I've already put them all away."

Jessie and Violet exchanged glances. Why was Mrs. Blackwell so secretive?

When Mrs. Blackwell had shown them the whole house, she led them back to the front hall. "I appreciate your help. If you need me, I'll be unpacking in my room," Mrs. Blackwell said, going up the stairs.

The Aldens looked around at the many boxes, wondering where to begin. Jessie spoke first. She was always very organized. "Henry and I will move the largest boxes. Violet can take the medium-sized ones, and Benny the small ones."

Benny frowned. "I can carry big boxes, too! I'm strong!"

Jessie smiled. "Yes, you are, Benny. But this way, we have a system."

Each of the Aldens picked up a box. "Library," said Henry, reading the label on the top of his box.

"Mine goes in the office," Jessie said, heading upstairs.

Violet and Benny each picked up a box for the living room.

The children worked steadily. It was hard work but they enjoyed it. Sometimes two of the Aldens would carry an especially heavy box together. As they moved the boxes, they made a game of guessing what might be inside each one.

"This box must be full of books," said

Jessie, picking up a heavy box labeled *Library*.

"And this one must be full of rocks!" said Benny, groaning as he lifted another.

Jessie came to a box with a red mark on it. "What did Mrs. Blackwell say about these?"

"She said to be very careful with them," Violet reminded her. "They have something to do with Mr. Blackwell's work and they go in the back hallway."

"What do you think that red mark means?" Benny wondered.

"It looks like an hourglass," said Jessie.

"An hourglass is an old-fashioned clock," Violet said, noticing Benny's puzzled face. "Maybe Mr. Blackwell works on old clocks and that's what's in these boxes."

"That would explain why we need to be careful with them," said Jessie. "Old clocks and hourglasses can be fragile."

Henry had been standing silently, staring at the red marking.

"What is it, Henry?" Violet asked.

"I don't know," Henry said. "But that red hourglass reminds me of something. I wish I could remember what."

While they were talking, the telephone rang. Mrs. Blackwell came down the stairs quickly. "Now where did I plug in the phone?" she said to herself, looking around the piles of boxes and wads of crumpled paper.

They could all hear the insistent ringing, but the phone was nowhere to be seen.

"Here it is," Violet said, pulling the phone from behind a box.

"Thanks," Mrs. Blackwell said. "Hello?" she said into the receiver. She walked into the living room, away from the kids.

The Aldens went back to their work.

Benny didn't intend to eavesdrop on Mrs. Blackwell's conversation, but as he carried a box to the dining room, he couldn't help hearing her words. "I'm on the trail, but I haven't tracked them down yet," she said into the phone.

Mrs. Blackwell stopped talking and listened to the person on the other end. She

seemed to be getting upset. Her face was turning red and when she spoke, her voice was loud and angry. Now all the children heard what she was saying. "I know, I know! Time is running out. But I have to set it up just right . . . They can't know I'm there."

There was silence again as Mrs. Blackwell listened to the caller. She seemed calmer when she spoke again. "Don't worry. I'll be sure to catch them in the act."

Benny was paying so much attention to what Mrs. Blackwell was saying that he dropped the box he was holding. Mrs. Blackwell turned around and saw him staring at her. She quickly spoke into the receiver. "I can't talk right now — I'll call you back later." She hung up the phone.

Embarrassed, Benny and the others quickly got busy, picking up boxes and reading their labels. Mrs. Blackwell headed back up the stairs.

Once she was gone, the Aldens clustered together in the hallway. "What was she talking about?" asked Benny in a hushed voice.

"When she said she had a unique job,"

Jessie said, "I didn't realize she meant one that involves secretly tracking people down!"

"And catching them 'in the act,' " Violet added. "What do you think that means?"

"Maybe she's a police officer and she needs to catch some suspects while they're committing a crime," said Henry.

"She could be a detective," suggested Jessie.

"Or a spy!" said Benny, his eyes wide. "A secret agent! That would explain why she seems so mysterious!"

"That also might explain why she has those high walls all around the house and how she always knows we're coming before we even ring the bell," Henry added. "Maybe she has some kind of hidden cameras posted at the front walk."

"I sure felt like I was being watched," Benny said, sounding excited.

"Maybe that red hourglass has something to do with it," Violet said. "Maybe her husband is a spy, too, and they keep their special equipment in those boxes."

"Yeah, the red hourglass could be their secret code," said Jessie.

"We should definitely keep our eyes and ears open while we're here," said Henry. "Neighbors who might be secret agents — now *that's* worth investigating!"

After the children had been working for about an hour, Mrs. Blackwell came back downstairs. "My goodness!" she said. "You've cleared out all the boxes down here! You are good workers, just as you said."

"We like to work hard," said Henry.

"I hadn't realized you'd be done with those boxes so quickly," Mrs. Blackwell said. "I think I can handle the rest on my own."

The Aldens looked at one another. If they left now, they'd never find out if the Blackwells were spies.

"There must be something else we can help with," said Henry.

"Well, if you're sure you don't mind . . ." Mrs. Blackwell thought for a minute and then began walking toward the library. "You could help shelve the books."

The library was a dark room at the back of the house. The walls were lined with bookcases reaching from floor to ceiling. The floor was cluttered with large stacks of boxes — some the children had carried in that morning, others had been brought in earlier.

"We have so many books," Mrs. Blackwell said.

"You sure do," Benny said, looking around at all the boxes.

"I have an idea!" Jessie said. "We could organize the books — you know, like at the library. We'll divide them into different categories, like fiction or nonfiction. Then we'll shelve them in alphabetical order."

A smile spread across Mrs. Blackwell's face. "That sounds wonderful."

Now it was Jessie's turn to smile. "Great! We'll get right to work."

As soon as Mrs. Blackwell had left, Jessie came up with a plan. "We'll put the books in piles, depending on what they're about. Then we'll alphabetize them and put them on the shelves." She opened a box and pulled out a book. "*Top Secret Spies from Around the Globe*," she read from the cover.

"Really?" asked Benny. "A book about spies?"

"Here's another one," said Violet. "*The World's Greatest Spies*."

"I've got one in this box, too," said Henry, holding up a book. "*A Secret Agent's Guide to Gadgets and Tools*."

Violet dug through the box of books in front of her. "Looks like a lot of the books in this box are spy books," she said.

"Just like I said!" Benny cried. "The Blackwells are spies!"

"I think you're jumping to conclusions," Henry said. "Although they certainly do have a lot of spy books."

Benny opened another box. "This doesn't look like a spy book," he said, looking at the book on top. "This one has a spider on the cover." He pulled out the book underneath. "That's weird," he said. "Another one about spiders."

Henry looked over Benny's shoulder and read the book's title aloud. "*The Complete*

Book of Spiders." He opened another box. "This one has some spider books, too!"

"We'd better stop talking and start sorting," said Jessie. "Otherwise we'll never get done in here. This pile over here will be for spy books, and this one for spider books."

"Spies and spiders. The Blackwells sure are interested in some unusual things," said Henry.

CHAPTER 3

The Red Glow

The Aldens spent the rest of the morning unpacking books and putting them in piles. When they had emptied a box, they unfolded it and stacked the flattened cardboard in a pile in the corner.

They had just unpacked the last box of books when Violet looked up and saw Mrs. Blackwell standing in the doorway, watching them.

"Oh!" Violet said, surprised. "I didn't hear you come in. How long have you been standing there?"

Mrs. Blackwell raised an eyebrow. "A little while. I came in quietly."

That's for sure, thought Violet. Mrs. Blackwell hadn't made a sound.

"Why don't you take a break?" Mrs. Blackwell suggested.

Jessie looked at the piles of books all around them. "But we aren't done. . . ." She hated to leave a job incomplete.

"That's okay, you can finish this later," Mrs. Blackwell said.

"I *am* getting kind of hungry," Henry said.

"Me, too!" cried Benny.

"That's no surprise," said Violet. Their little brother was always ready to eat.

"We'll come back after lunch," Jessie said.

"See you then," said Mrs. Blackwell. She turned quickly and disappeared down the dark hallway, leaving the Aldens alone.

The Aldens let themselves out of the Blackwells' house. They were happy to be outside in the bright sunshine. "It's so dark in there," Violet said as she led the way down the driveway.

"And that's not even the strangest thing," Jessie said. "Those things Mrs. Blackwell was saying on the telephone . . . the way she appeared so silently in the library . . . all those books about spiders and secret agents."

"I think it's cool," said Benny. "We've never had neighbors who were spies before."

"Do you really think they're spies?" Violet asked.

"I suppose they could be," said Henry. "Mrs. Blackwell said she and her husband have unique jobs. But spies . . ." His voice trailed off doubtfully.

Benny, however, was sure. "I wonder what their secret mission is!" he said. "Maybe there are bad guys right here in Greenfield. Maybe they're out to take over the world!"

The others smiled as Benny became more and more carried away. "Maybe the Blackwells are going to catch the bad guys and — "

Suddenly Benny stopped talking. He'd

spotted something strange. A man was sitting in a dark blue car parked on the side of the road, across from the Blackwells' front gate. As the Aldens walked up the street, he turned his head to watch them go by.

"Hey, you guys," Benny whispered. "The man in that car is watching us!"

"Uh-oh," Jessie said, opening her eyes wide and smiling at her brother. "Is he another spy?"

Henry laughed. "An international spy ring is taking over Greenfield!"

Benny frowned. "No, really, he's watching us!"

Henry put his arm around his brother. "I think you're getting a little carried away."

Benny shrugged off his brother's arm. "I am *not*!"

Violet had turned to study the man in the blue car. The man noticed her looking at him. He started the car and drove off down the street. Violet gasped. "Henry, wait! The man's license plate — it says SPIDER2!"

"No way!" said Jessie. "What a strange license plate!"

SPIDER 2

"Spiders on the gates and spiders on the plates," Henry rhymed. Violet and Jessie laughed.

Benny cracked a smile. Maybe Henry was right. Maybe he *was* taking the spy idea too seriously. "Last one home gets spiders for lunch!" he shouted and raced off down the sidewalk.

After a delicious meal of Mrs. MacGregor's tuna casserole, the Aldens went back to the Blackwells'. They stood among the piles of books in the library. The largest pile held books about spiders and insects. Next to that was a large stack of books about secret agents and spies. There was also a whole collection of mystery novels.

"The Blackwells like mysteries, just like us!" said Benny as he stacked up the novels.

"Look at all these dictionaries," Violet said, pulling a German dictionary from under a French one. "The Blackwells must speak a lot of languages."

"You have to know a lot of languages if you're a spy," Benny said.

"Not that again," said Jessie. "We've got a job to do here — we can't keep talking about spies."

"And we wouldn't want Mrs. Blackwell to come in and hear us talking about that," Violet added.

"About what?" said Mrs. Blackwell. Again she had appeared in the door silently.

The Aldens didn't know what to say.

Mrs. Blackwell looked at them, waiting for an answer.

"Oh, um . . ." Jessie stammered.

Mrs. Blackwell stared at them for several more seconds. At last she spoke. "Never mind. I just came to say that I have some important work to do this afternoon and it is important that I not be disturbed. Do you think you'll be able to finish all these books today?"

"Oh, yes," said Violet. "I'm sure we can."

Mrs. Blackwell smiled. "Then I'll count on it. It will be a great relief to be able to use my library again. When you're done just let yourselves out the front door, and I'll see you tomorrow."

"Okay," said Henry as Mrs. Blackwell headed back upstairs.

"She sure does come in unexpectedly," said Violet.

"You have to be able to sneak around when you're a spy," Benny said.

Jessie gave her little brother a scolding look. "Which is exactly why we'd better watch what we talk about while we're here."

She bent and picked up several dictionaries. "I'm going to put these right near the desk. That way they're easy to reach if you need to look something up." As Jessie lined up one dictionary after another, she said, "You know it's true, you *would* need to know a lot of languages if you were an international secret agent."

"There are other explanations for knowing lots of languages," Henry pointed out. "Maybe they own an international business."

"Or maybe they like to travel," added Violet.

"Speaking of travel, look at this," said Jessie. She had just picked up a large, well-worn book. The other children crowded around her.

"What is it?" asked Henry.

"It's an atlas — a book of maps. Look at all the pages that have been tagged," Jessie said, flipping the pages. Several pages were marked with small yellow tags. Notes were scribbled on some of the tags, but the handwriting was messy and hard to read.

"Maybe those tags show where the Blackwells have traveled," Violet suggested.

"Or the locations of their international factories," said Henry.

"Or maybe those are the places where they've gone on secret missions!" Benny said.

Jessie looked more closely at one of the tags stuck on a map of the United States. Slowly she sounded out the words. "This tag says *Lactrodectus hesperus*. And there's another one that says *Lactrodectus mactans*." She frowned. "What in the world do those words mean?"

"Sounds like the code name for a secret mission to me!" Benny said.

Henry and Violet chuckled and went back to work. But Jessie looked thoughtful. She took a pen and a small piece of paper from Mrs. Blackwell's desk and copied the words written on the tags. She put the atlas on the bookshelf.

Next, Jessie looked at the dictionaries. Finding a regular English dictionary, she pulled it out and flipped the pages of words that start with L to where *Lactrodectus* would appear. She ran her finger down the page, looking for the definition of Lactrodectus. She was disappointed to see that the word wasn't there. Next she looked up *hesperus*. That wasn't in the dictionary either. Neither was *mactans*. Puzzled, Jessie returned the dictionary to the shelf.

"What are you doing, Jessie?" Violet asked.

"I was hoping to find out what these words mean," Jessie said. "But they aren't in the dictionary."

Violet looked thoughtfully at the shelf of dictionaries. Suddenly, she had an idea. She pulled a French dictionary from the shelf.

"Did you look in this one, Jessie? Maybe those words are in a foreign language."

Jessie smiled. "Good thinking, Violet!"

The girls set to work looking up the words in the foreign dictionaries. They weren't in the French dictionary. Jessie pulled out the German dictionary, then the Italian one. "No luck," she said.

They went through one dictionary after another but the mysterious words were nowhere to be found.

Putting the last dictionary back on the shelf, Jessie sighed.

"That's weird," said Violet.

"Yeah," Jessie said. She shrugged and tucked the scrap of paper with the mystery words in her backpack. "Let's get back to work."

By mid-afternoon, the Aldens had filled the four bottom shelves of each bookcase with neatly arranged books. But even Henry was having trouble reaching the higher shelves.

"I'll go ask Mrs. Blackwell if she has a step-ladder," said Jessie, starting out the door.

"Remember, she said not to bother her," Violet called.

Jessie stopped in her tracks. "That's right."

"If we look around, I'm sure we can find a stool somewhere or a box sturdy enough to stand on," Henry said.

The Aldens walked all around the downstairs. There were no stools or stepladders in sight. The chairs they found were either too large to move or too delicate to stand on.

The children returned to the library and looked at the stacks of books they still had to shelve. "We can't just leave them like this," said Jessie.

"Maybe we *should* find Mrs. Blackwell," said Benny.

"No, she said it was important not to bother her," Henry said firmly.

"What can we do?" asked Violet. "She also said she's counting on us to finish this today."

The Aldens stood silently for a moment, thinking. Then Jessie spoke. "I'll go upstairs and take a quick peek around. Maybe there's a stool up there. I won't bother Mrs. Blackwell."

Jessie went quickly up the stairs while the others waited in the library. "Hello?" she called softly. She didn't want to bother Mrs. Blackwell, but she also didn't want to intrude on her without warning. It was eerily silent upstairs. "That's strange," Jessie muttered to herself. "It feels so empty up here." She quickened her pace.

Jessie peeked cautiously into the study. There was no sign of Mrs. Blackwell. As she turned to leave the room, Jessie spotted a small stepstool in the corner. "That's what we need," she said to herself. She picked up the stool and was about to go back downstairs when she noticed a strange light coming from the sitting room. It looked as if something inside the room was giving off a red glow. Jessie walked slowly into the room.

Off the sitting room was a tightly closed door. Above the door was a single bare lightbulb. The light was glowing red.

Was that there before? Jessie wondered. *No,* she told herself. *Or if it was, it wasn't turned on. I would have remembered that strange glow.* Jessie *did* remember the door the light was over. She had asked about the door when Mrs. Blackwell gave them the tour of the house that morning. Mrs. Blackwell hadn't answered the question about what was behind it.

Jessie picked up the stool and hurried out of the room. She was suddenly anxious to be back downstairs with her sister and brothers.

"You found one!" Violet said when Jessie returned with the stepstool.

"Yes," said Jessie, putting it down. She felt calmer now that she was back in the library.

"Did you see Mrs. Blackwell?" Henry asked.

"No, I didn't see or hear her anywhere," said Jessie. "But I did see something else."

"What?" Benny asked, instantly curious.

"Remember that door off the sitting room?" Jessie asked.

"You mean the one that Mrs. Blackwell didn't show us because she'd already put the boxes away?" Henry said.

"Exactly. That door was still closed and there was a weird red light over it," Jessie told them.

"Huh," said Henry, shrugging. "I guess they like colored lights." He picked up the stool, placed it close to the bookshelves, and climbed the two steps. Violet carried over some books and began handing them up to him.

"I don't think that's it," said Jessie. "There aren't colored lights anywhere else in the house. That light was weird. It seemed almost like a warning light."

"A warning about what?" asked Benny.

"I don't know," Jessie answered. "A warning not to enter that room, I guess."

"Maybe that's her office," Violet suggested. "She did say she had work to do and didn't want to be bothered."

"But have you ever seen an office with a warning light outside?" Jessie asked.

"It is a little unusual," Henry agreed. "But it wouldn't be the first unusual thing we've found here."

The others went back to shelving books, but Jessie just stood there, lost in thought.

It was close to dinnertime when the Aldens finished with the library. They stood back to admire the shelves and shelves of neatly arranged books.

"Looks great," said Henry, "if I do say so myself."

The children left the stepstool in the library and let themselves out, as Mrs. Blackwell had instructed. The house was dark and silent. Henry pulled the front door shut behind them.

As they walked down the driveway, the Aldens noticed a man standing near the street. He had brown hair and was wearing a brown leather jacket. He was staring at the Blackwells' house as if deep in thought.

"Hello," called Henry. "May we help you?"

The man seemed startled to see the Aldens. He looked at them without saying a word, then began walking quickly down the street toward a car parked at the curb.

The Aldens reached the end of the driveway. "Is there anything — " Henry called out, but the man was already in his car, closing the door. A moment later, he had driven away.

"That was strange," said Henry, looking up the street in the direction the car had gone. "He hurried away the minute he saw us."

"Without even saying hello," Violet added.

"He seemed very interested in the Blackwells' house," Jessie said.

"And you know what's even stranger?" Benny said. "That was the same man we saw at lunchtime, the one who was watching us from his car."

"Are you sure?" Violet asked.

"Yes," said Benny. "SPIDER2."

CHAPTER 4

Lights at Night

Over dinner that night, the children told Grandfather all about the mysterious Blackwells and the mystery man. When they reached the end of their story, Benny started to giggle.

"What's so funny?" Jessie wanted to know.

"The Blackwells are spies," said Benny. "And now someone's spying on them!"

"I can't help wondering if that man has anything to do with what Mrs. Blackwell said on the phone," said Jessie. "Could he be the one Mrs. Blackwell is tracking?"

"We don't know for sure that Mrs. Blackwell is tracking someone," Violet pointed out.

"Violet is right," Grandfather agreed. "Mrs. Blackwell's phone call does sound surprising, but I'm sure there's a simple explanation."

"Really?" Benny asked. "Like what?"

Grandfather thought for a moment. "I'm not sure," he admitted. "But I wouldn't worry about it. Hearing one side of a telephone conversation always sounds odd."

The Aldens finished their dinner, then Henry and Violet cleared the table and Jessie and Benny washed the dishes. When the kitchen was clean, the children joined Grandfather in the living room. They played checkers and read books until it was time for bed. Saying good night, they each headed into their own rooms.

Henry walked over to the windows in his room to pull down his shades when something outside caught his eye. From the window next to his bed, Henry could see the side of the Blackwells' house. Because

Henry's bedroom was on the second floor, he could see over the tall stone wall that surrounded the Blackwells' property.

Henry studied the side of the house. On the first floor was a long row of windows. "That must be the room down the hallway where Mr. Blackwell works," he said to himself. The shades on the windows were drawn, but the lights inside were on. Henry could see the shadow of someone moving around inside.

Henry looked at his clock. It was nine o'clock and Mr. Blackwell was still at work. That seemed unusual. Grandfather sometimes worked late, but he was usually finished before nine. "I wonder what kind of work Mr. Blackwell does," Henry wondered aloud. He pulled the shade down firmly.

Henry put on his pajamas and brushed his teeth. Checking the window again, he saw that Mr. Blackwell's light was still on. He slid into bed and picked up his book. After reading a chapter, Henry sat up and peeked out the window. The light was still shining. Henry closed his book and turned off his lamp. "Tomorrow we'll go back to the Blackwells'," he murmured sleepily. "Tomorrow we'll find some answers."

Several hours later, Henry woke up with a jolt. A noise outside had awakened him. It came again — a long, mournful howl.

Henry gasped as his bedroom door suddenly swung open. Then he relaxed. It was Violet.

"Did you hear that noise outside?" Violet asked softly.

Henry nodded. The howl came again. "I think it's a cat," he said.

"Do you think it's hurt?" Violet asked, sounding worried. She walked over to the window next to Henry's bed and lifted the shade. The two children peered out into the dark yard, trying to see the cat. "I don't see anything," said Violet.

"I do," Henry replied. "Look." He pointed to the Blackwells' house. The house was dark except for the light coming through one window on the first floor. Behind the drawn window shade was the shadow of a person.

"I think that's Mr. Blackwell's study," Henry told Violet. "He's been up working all night."

Violet's eyes popped open in surprise. She glanced at Henry's alarm clock. "But it's three o'clock in the morning!" she said. "What could he be working on at this hour?"

Henry shook his head and settled back into bed. "I don't know, Violet," he said. "But we're good detectives. Maybe we can find out tomorrow."

The next day, as the Aldens walked to the Blackwells' house, Henry and Violet told the others about seeing Mr. Blackwell working all night.

"Wow, they keep some late hours," said Jessie.

"Whatever their secret mission is, it must be super urgent," Benny said, sounding excited.

They were approaching the Blackwells' fence when a white car pulled up to the curb ahead of them. A man got out of the car and stepped out onto the sidewalk. He had dark, wavy hair and a small, well-trimmed beard. The man was holding a large piece of paper and looking up and down the street.

"I wonder if that man's lost," said Violet. "It looks as if he's checking a map."

When the Aldens reached the man, Henry said, "Excuse me, do you need help?"

The man looked startled. He quickly rolled up the paper and tucked it under his arm. Turning to face the children, he smiled broadly. "Hello!"

"We saw you were looking at a map," Jessie said. "Perhaps we can help you. We live around here."

"A map?" The man looked confused. Then he seemed to understand. He waved the rolled-up paper under his arm. "Oh, yes, this." He shook his head. "No, I'm not lost, but thanks for offering." He put out his hand to shake Henry's. "I'm Joe Toll."

"Hello," said Henry. "I'm Henry Alden. These are my sisters and brother."

"You said you live around here?" Joe Toll asked.

"Yes, right up the street, Mr. Toll," said Henry.

"Call me Joe," the man said with a smile. "Seems like a nice neighborhood."

"Yes, it is," said Henry.

"How about your neighbors? Nice people?" Joe wanted to know.

"Yes," said Jessie, raising one eyebrow. "Our neighbors are very nice. Why?"

"How about the people in this house here?" Joe motioned to the Blackwells'. "You seem to be headed in that direction. Do you know them well?"

"Not really," Henry replied. "They just moved in."

"Oh, they did?" asked Joe. "Did they just build the house?"

Benny spoke up. "You sure have a lot of questions! How come you want to know so much?"

For a moment Joe looked uncomfortable. "Me? Oh, I just . . ." His voice trailed off. Then he smiled. He gestured toward the

Blackwells' front gate. "I was just admiring this nice spider gate," he said. "I'm interested in spiders and I, uh, I wondered what kind of people would have a gate like that."

Henry nodded slowly. For some reason he didn't quite believe Joe.

"We're about to go see them," said Benny.

"You could go with us and we'll introduce you," Jessie offered.

"Oh, I uh . . . um . . . since they just moved in, they must be very busy," Joe said quickly. All of a sudden he seemed nervous. "Gotta run!" He quickly got back in his car and drove off.

"How odd," said Henry.

"You said it," said Jessie. "I don't think he was telling us the truth."

"If he just wants to know about the gate, then why was he asking all those questions about our neighbors?" asked Benny.

"I have no idea," said Violet.

"He seemed especially interested in the Blackwells," Henry pointed out. "Just like that man yesterday."

Benny's eyes opened wide. "Maybe Joe Toll is a spy, too."

Henry ruffled Benny's hair. "Now you're starting to think *everyone's* a spy!"

"Not *everyone*," said Benny. "Grandfather's not a spy. And Mrs. MacGregor's not a spy!"

"It's weird he was looking at a map, since he says he wasn't lost," Violet pointed out.

"That is kind of odd," Jessie agreed.

"I wonder if it really was a map," Henry said. "I mean, most maps fold up, and he *rolled* that one."

"Maybe spy maps roll instead of fold," said Benny.

"And it looked like that paper was mostly white with only a bit of writing on it," Henry continued. "Maps usually have lots of colors and writing on them."

"Hey, look!" cried Benny, pointing to the sidewalk. He bent down and picked up a small piece of paper. "Joe must have dropped this."

"What does it say?" Henry asked.

Benny was just learning to read. He

sounded out the letters, "Bl . . . bl . . . black . . ." He took a breath. "Black-well. Hey! I think it says Blackwell!"

Henry looked over Benny's shoulder. "You're right. It does say Blackwell. And that's their address. I wonder why he'd have that, especially since it sounded as if he didn't know them."

The children were silent for a moment, wondering.

"I don't know," Violet said at last. "But maybe we'll find some answers inside."

"Come on, you guys," Jessie said. "Let's see if Mrs. Blackwell was pleased with the way we set up the books." She led the way to the door.

Mrs. Blackwell was very pleased with the books. As soon as the children came inside, she told them what a great job they'd done. "You organized the library really nicely."

Jessie beamed.

"It was a huge help to me last night when I had some research to do," Mrs. Blackwell went on.

"What kind of research?" asked Jessie. Mrs. Blackwell seemed a little friendlier than she had been before. Jessie hoped that meant she would answer the Aldens' questions.

"Oh, just something for my work," Mrs. Blackwell responded.

"Were you working late last night?" Henry asked, remembering the light he'd seen.

"No, I go to bed early," she answered. "I'm a morning person."

Violet and Henry exchanged glances. *Now we know that was* Mr. *Blackwell at three in the morning*, Henry thought. He didn't mention the light, however, because he didn't want Mrs. Blackwell to feel he was spying on her.

"Today it would be great if you could unpack the pots and the dishes," Mrs. Blackwell said, leading the way to the kitchen. "My husband and I are getting tired of eating take-out food."

In the kitchen, the boxes were stacked up against the cabinets and on the counters. There were large boxes filled with pots and pans and serving bowls, and smaller boxes of dishes, glasses, and silverware.

"Where would you like us to put everything?" Violet asked.

"You kids did such a good job in the library," Mrs. Blackwell said. "Why don't you arrange it the way you'd like."

"Okay!" said Jessie. She was pleased that Mrs. Blackwell trusted them with that responsibility.

"We'll get right to work," said Violet.

As she was walking out, Mrs. Blackwell noticed a box with a red marking on the top. "This one doesn't belong in here," she said to herself.

Jessie jumped at the opportunity to ask, "What does that marking mean anyway?"

"I told you, those boxes are my husband's," Mrs. Blackwell said.

"I was just wondering if that shape meant something," Jessie said.

"That shape?" Mrs. Blackwell seemed to be considering something. After a few seconds she said, "No. Nothing." As she turned to walk away, the phone rang. Mrs. Blackwell hesitated, then handed the box to Benny. "Could you take this to my husband, please? I'm going to answer that in the other room." She turned quickly and walked out.

Benny looked down at the box.

"I'll take that," Jessie said. "Mrs. Blackwell said to be very careful with those."

"*I* can be careful," Benny told her. "She asked *me* to take it."

Before Jessie could stop him, Benny walked out with the box. Although the box was small, it was a heavy one. He groaned softly so the others wouldn't hear and carried it to the back hall.

When Benny reached the hallway, he stopped and put the box down. He shook out his arms, which were tired from carrying the heavy box. "Now where do these marked boxes go?" he said to himself.

He looked down the hall. It was long, dark, and narrow. At the end was a closed door with a light glowing underneath. "That must be the place," Benny said to himself. It didn't look very welcoming.

Benny took a deep breath and began to walk slowly down the hallway toward the door, wondering what he would find behind it. When he got to the end of the hallway, Benny set the box down again. He looked at the closed door in front of him. Then he knocked softly on the door. There was no response, so he knocked a little bit louder. Still no response.

Benny cautiously tried the doorknob.

The door creaked open, revealing a brightly lit room.

A male voice called out angrily from within, "Please don't come in!"

"I'm sorry!" Benny said. He quickly shut the door. He hadn't seen who the voice belonged to. Mr. Blackwell must have been on the other side of the room, behind the door.

Benny had seen only one thing clearly before shutting the door. Next to the door was a large glass case.

Inside the case was a large web and the blackest spider Benny had ever seen.

CHAPTER 5

Following the Map

Benny turned around and was startled to find Mrs. Blackwell standing right behind him. "What are you doing?" she demanded.

"I, um, was just bringing the box back here," Benny said.

"Didn't I tell you not to go in there?" Mrs. Blackwell asked.

Benny gulped. Mrs. Blackwell looked very angry. "Yes," said Benny. "I'm sorry. I thought you wanted me to bring Mr. Blackwell this box."

Mrs. Blackwell stared at Benny for a moment, then her face softened. "You're right, Benny," she said. "I did say that. But what I meant was for you to leave the box in the hallway. I should have been more clear."

Benny stood still for a minute, unsure of what to do. Then he handed the box to Mrs. Blackwell. "I'm sorry," he repeated.

"It's okay, Benny," she said. "Just don't come near this room again."

Benny headed quickly back toward the kitchen. When he came to the end of the hallway he turned around and looked back. Mrs. Blackwell was standing motionless, watching him.

Benny was relieved when he reached the kitchen where his sisters and brother were unpacking a large box of dishes. He had been walking so quickly he was breathing heavily.

"What's the matter?" asked Violet. "You look as if you'd seen a ghost!"

"Not a ghost," Benny replied. "A spider."

"What?" asked Violet, putting down the stack of plates she was holding.

Benny told the others what had happened.

"Wow," said Henry when Benny had finished. "Cool." Henry loved finding bugs in the backyard.

"Yeah, but Mrs. Blackwell looked really mad to see me back there," said Benny.

"I wonder why it's so important not to go in that room," said Jessie.

"That seems to be where Mr. Blackwell works," Henry said. "You know how Grandfather doesn't like us to disturb him when he's working."

"Yes, but Grandfather doesn't get so upset," Jessie pointed out.

"Everybody's different," said Violet.

"What about that spider?" said Benny. "Who keeps a spider for a pet?"

"That depends," Henry said. "What kind of spider was it?"

"I don't know," Benny said. "A black one. Very black." He paused, remembering. "And it had a really messy web."

"As messy as your room?" Violet teased.

"My room isn't messy!" Benny said.

"Hmmm . . ." said Henry thoughtfully.

"What is it?" asked Jessie.

"I was just thinking about that science book I took out of the library a few weeks ago," Henry said. "It was all about spiders. I wish I still had it."

"The Blackwells have lots of books about spiders in their library," said Violet. "Remember?"

Henry smiled. "Why didn't I think of that? We'll check it out after we've unpacked these boxes."

An hour later the Aldens had finished organizing the kitchen. They looked with satisfaction at the cabinets filled with neatly stacked dishes and carefully placed cups.

"We can go into the library now," said Jessie. "We've earned a break anyway."

The Aldens walked quickly to the library. Most of the spider books were on a high shelf. Henry climbed up on the stepstool and searched for a book that would be useful. Jessie looked around the room. She spotted something on the desk.

"Hey, you guys, take a look at this," Jessie said.

Henry climbed down from the stool. The Aldens huddled together around the desk.

"What is it?" Henry asked, looking down at the paper Jessie had spotted. Someone had drawn a diagram on the paper, with several rectangles and lines.

"Looks like a map," said Jessie.

"A map of what?" asked Violet.

"A treasure map?" Benny asked hopefully.

The Aldens stood silently looking at the map for several minutes. Suddenly, Violet said, "Wait a minute . . ." She took another look at the map, then ran to the window. The library was at the back of the house. From the window she could see a large, curved stone patio. Beyond the patio was a big yard ringed with tall grass and woods.

"That's it!" Violet cried.

She ran back to the map. "This is a map of the backyard. The large rectangle is the house." She pointed to the bottom of the diagram. "See, this curve matches the curve of the patio. So this smaller rectangle is the shed. These lines represent the tall grass out there."

"And what is that X?" asked Henry.

Violet slowly shook her head. "I have no idea. I don't see anything out the window."

"It's obvious," said Benny. "An X on a map *always* means treasure. Doesn't it?"

"I'm curious," said Jessie.

"There's only one way to find out," said Henry. "Let's go."

"We can't just go poking around in the backyard!" said Violet. "What will we tell Mrs. Blackwell?"

"The truth," said Henry. "That we'd like to take a look at her backyard. I'm sure she won't mind."

The children considered this plan. "All right," said Jessie. "I don't see any harm in it."

Leaving the map on the desk in the library, the Aldens went back to the main hallway. "Mrs. Blackwell?" Jessie called up the stairs.

"Yes?" came a voice from above.

"We've finished unpacking the kitchen," Jessie said.

"Very good," said Mrs. Blackwell, appearing at the top of the stairs. "You do work quickly."

"We were wondering if we could take a little break and get some fresh air in your backyard," said Henry.

"That would be fine," Mrs. Blackwell said.

The Aldens went out the back door into the spacious yard. "Wow," said Benny. "This would be a great place to play baseball."

"It would be," Jessie agreed. "But that's not what we're here for. Now, what did that map say?"

"The X was just beyond the tall grass," said Henry.

"That's the grass over there," Violet said, pointing.

The Aldens walked across the yard to where the grass grew tall and wild. They looked around but could see nothing unusual. "Maybe it's on the other side of the grass," Violet said, pushing her way through.

"I don't know what we're looking for, but I don't see anything out of the ordinary," said Jessie, crawling into the grass.

"Maybe something is buried out here," suggested Benny. "That's how they always do it in books."

"But if something was buried here recently, we'd see an area that looked freshly dug up," said Henry. "I don't see anything like that."

"Neither do I," said Jessie. "And if it was buried a long time ago, it could be anywhere." She was disappointed. "Maybe we read the map wrong. Let's go back and look again."

The Aldens walked across the wide yard and through the back door. They had just stepped inside when they heard Mrs. Blackwell's voice. "Stop right there! Don't move!"

CHAPTER 6

Beware the Spider's Bite

Mrs. Blackwell was rushing down the stairs, a look of horror on her face. She headed straight for Jessie.

"What is it?" asked Henry.

"On Jessie's back!" said Mrs. Blackwell.

Jessie froze and the other Aldens turned to look. In the middle of Jessie's back was the largest spider the children had ever seen.

Before the Aldens could react, Mrs. Blackwell plucked the spider off of Jessie. Cupping it delicately in her hands, she

spoke in a gentle voice. "My poor girl!"

Jessie rubbed her back with her hand to brush off the feeling of the spider. She smiled and was about to speak when she realized Mrs. Blackwell hadn't been talking to her at all. She was talking to the spider!

Mrs. Blackwell looked down into her cupped hands. "Were you hitching a ride on Jessie's back?" she cooed in the same gentle tone. "Good thing I spotted you out the window!"

The Aldens clustered around to see the spider. It was three inches long, with thin legs and a black and yellow egg-shaped body. Mrs. Blackwell walked quickly out the back door and across the yard. She placed the spider in the high grass where the children had been.

When Mrs. Blackwell stepped back into the house, she seemed surprised to see all the children staring at her in amazement. "What's the matter?" she asked. "It was just a yellow garden spider. They can't hurt you."

"B-b-but — " Jessie stuttered.

"It was huge!" said Benny.

"Why are people always so concerned with size?" muttered Mrs. Blackwell. "That has nothing to do with how dangerous a spider is. That poor spider was just looking for a place to make a web and accidentally ended up on Jessie's back."

"Really?" said Violet.

"Yes. Yellow garden spiders like to build their nests in places like that tall grass," Mrs. Blackwell said. "What were you doing back there anyway?"

The children looked at each other, unsure what to say. "We were just exploring," Henry said at last.

"How do you know so much about spiders?" asked Benny.

"I've always been fascinated by spiders, ever since I was young," Mrs. Blackwell said. She looked off into the distance, a soft smile on her face as she remembered. "I used to go out in the yard to look for them."

"Neat!" said Violet, trying to picture Mrs. Blackwell as a young girl. "And so you still like spiders?"

"I do," Mrs. Blackwell said.

Violet was about to ask something else when Benny interrupted her. "Does Mr. Blackwell like spiders, too? Is that why he keeps that spider in the room at the back of the house?"

Suddenly the smile disappeared from Mrs. Blackwell's face. "Please don't go back there again," she said, then turned and walked toward the study.

"Mrs. Blackwell," Henry called after her. "Would you mind if we stopped working now and came back tomorrow? We'd like to visit the public library this afternoon."

"That's fine," said Mrs. Blackwell, barely turning around.

Violet looked disappointed. "She was just starting to talk to us, to be friendly," she whispered. "I wish you hadn't asked her about that spider, Benny."

"I didn't know it would make her stop talking to us," Benny said.

"I wonder why it did," Jessie said.

The Aldens checked to make sure that everything had been put away neatly in the kitchen. Then they left the Blackwells' house and headed home for a quick lunch. While Jessie boiled some hot dogs, Henry got out buns, ketchup, and mustard. Benny took out four plates and napkins and Violet poured four large cups of milk.

"Let's eat our lunch in the boxcar," suggested Benny.

"Great idea," said Violet. She placed the cups of milk on a tray and led the way to the backyard. Watch scampered around the children's feet as they walked.

Soon they were sitting inside the boxcar, munching their hot dogs. Watch sat quietly in a corner, chewing a bone.

"So we never did find out what that map was for," Henry said in between bites.

"All it led us to was a spider," said Benny.

"Maybe that's what the map was for!" said Violet excitedly.

"I thought it was a treasure map," said Benny. "Spiders aren't treasure."

"But don't you see?" Violet said. "That's exactly what spiders *are* to Mrs. Blackwell."

"I still think there's more she's not telling us," said Jessie.

After they'd finished eating, the children set off for the library on their bikes. Henry led them straight to the section with books about spiders and insects. "Here's the book I took out last month," he said, pulling the book from a shelf. The cover showed a large photograph of a brown spider.

Henry flipped it open. He turned each page slowly, studying the photographs. His brother and sisters peered over his shoulder.

"Hey look!" cried Benny, pointing to a picture in the book. "That looks like the spider that was on Jessie's back."

Jessie shivered. Benny was right. The black and yellow spider in the photograph looked just like the one Mrs. Blackwell had taken off her back.

Violet leaned closer and studied the text under the photograph. "It says this spider goes by lots of different names. Yellow Garden Spider — that's what Mrs. Blackwell called it. I like this name: Golden Orb Weaver."

"What does that say?" asked Benny, pointing to some italicized words written in smaller print.

"*Argiope aurantia*," Henry read, slowly sounding out the difficult words. "It says that's the spider's scientific name."

Henry continued flipping the pages until he came to a full-page photograph of a very black spider. "Wait!" he said. "This might be it." He read quietly to himself while the others waited. Then he said, "I found it!"

"What?" asked Jessie.

"Listen to this." Henry began reading from the book. " 'One of the most well-known spiders is the black widow spider. This spider can be identified by its inky black coloring and the red hourglass marking on the female's underside.' "

"Red hourglass marking!" cried Violet. "Just like on the boxes!"

"Yes," said Henry. "I knew that red symbol reminded me of something."

"What does *widow* mean?" asked Benny.

"A widow is a woman whose husband has died," Henry explained. "It says here the black widow spider has that name because the female is much larger and sometimes eats the male."

"Really?" said Benny. "That's not very nice."

"No," Henry said. "It isn't. But it says the males sometimes escape after throwing strands of silk at the females. Look, here's a picture." He held the book so the others could see.

"Hey!" said Benny. "That looks like the spider I saw in the glass case!"

"It does?" Violet asked.

"Yes," said Benny. "I didn't see an hourglass, but the spider was really black, with long legs. And its web was all tangled like that one in the picture. Remember, I told you it was messy."

"What else does the book say about black widows?" Jessie asked.

"Let's see," said Henry. He began to read aloud again. " 'The black widow spider bites if it feels threatened. Its poison is extremely strong — fifteen times stronger than that of a rattlesnake.' " Henry paused and looked around at the others. "Wow."

"The poison is fifteen times stronger than a rattlesnake's?" Jessie repeated.

Henry nodded.

"No wonder Mrs. Blackwell doesn't want us in that back room!" said Violet.

"Now I *really* wonder why someone would keep that spider as a pet!" said Benny.

Henry was just about to close up the book when Jessie spotted something. "Let me see that book for a minute," she said.

Henry handed the book to her. Jessie pointed to the word she had spotted. She said it aloud slowly, "*Lactrodectus.*"

"What's that?" asked Violet.

"I guess it's the scientific name for black widow spiders," Jessie said. "But it's also one of the words . . ."

"Written on a tag in the Blackwell's atlas!" cried Violet.

Jessie was unzipping her backpack. She pulled out the piece of paper she'd tucked in there earlier. "*Lactrodectus hesperus, Lactrodectus mactans.*" Jessie looked back at the spider book. She read aloud, " 'The species

Lactrodectus hesperus is found in the Western United States, while *Lactrodectus mactans* is common to the Eastern and Central United States.' "

"So that's why they had those tags stuck on the maps — different kinds of spiders live in different places," said Violet.

"Why would the Blackwells label where spiders live in their atlas?" asked Henry. "That's a pretty weird hobby."

"Unless they use spider code names for their spy missions!" said Benny.

The others shrugged, still unsure.

"I'm just glad we figured out what those strange words are," Violet said.

"And now I see why they weren't in the dictionary — they're scientific terms," said Jessie.

Henry brought the spider book to the checkout counter. He wanted to take it home to read more. When the librarian saw the book she said, "If you're interested in spiders, you should visit the new exhibit at the Greenfield Museum." She pointed to a flyer tacked onto the bulletin board. SPI-

DERS AND OTHER ARACHNIDS, the flyer read. STARTS TUESDAY AT THE GREENFIELD MUSEUM. PET A TARANTULA. HOLD A SCORPION. LEARN HOW SPIDERS WEAVE THEIR WEBS.

"Look, you guys," said Henry, pointing to the flyer. "A spider exhibit at the Greenfield Museum."

Benny smiled. "Let's check it out!"

"It starts tomorrow," Jessie said.

"Then that's when we'll go!" said Henry. The Aldens headed out the door of the library toward the bike rack where they had left their bikes.

The Aldens were peddling down their street when they saw two men coming out of the Blackwells' house. Henry, who was leading the way, slowed his bike to a stop. His brother and sisters braked behind him. "Look," Henry said softly. "Isn't that Joe Toll, the guy with the map that wasn't a map?"

Violet nodded. "I think so," she whispered. "And look who he's with!"

Benny's eyes widened in amazement. "That's the guy from the SPIDER2 car!"

The Aldens watched silently as the two men walked down the driveway. Both men looked unhappy, as if something bad had just happened.

"I can't believe they weren't interested," the man from the car was saying. "Not for any amount of money."

"That's not true," said Joe. "They said they'd think about our offer. I think we can convince them."

The men had reached the Blackwells' spider gate. They hadn't noticed the Aldens across the street. As the men walked away from the children, toward their car, Henry caught a glimpse of the back of Joe's jacket.

His jaw dropped open.

"What is it?" Violet asked.

"Joe's jacket," Henry said softly.

The others looked to see what had shocked Henry. Sewn into the back of the man's jacket was a picture of a scary-looking spider. Above it were the words, BEWARE THE SPIDER'S BITE.

CHAPTER 7

The Bracelet

"Weird," said Violet. "That can't be just a coincidence."

"We *have* been seeing a lot of spiders lately," said Benny.

"How could I forget," Jessie said, rubbing her back.

"Besides the ones on your back and Joe's back, there's the design on the Blackwells' gate," Violet said.

"And the one I saw in the glass case," Benny added.

"And the red hourglass symbol on the boxes," Violet said.

Henry had been silent while the others were talking.

"Henry, what are you thinking about?" Violet asked him.

Henry was startled out of his thoughts. "What?"

Violet smiled. "I asked what you were thinking about."

"Oh — I don't know. The words on Joe's jacket, 'Beware the Spider's Bite.' That sounds so familiar," Henry explained.

"Really? Why?" asked Jessie.

Henry shook his head. "That's what I've been thinking about. I can't remember."

"What do you think those guys were doing at the Blackwells' house?" asked Benny.

"I don't know, but they didn't look happy," said Violet.

"They said they made the Blackwells some sort of 'offer,' which the Blackwells refused," Jessie recalled. "Joe said he thought he could convince them."

"That must be why Joe had the Blackwells' name on that piece of paper we found," Violet said. "He was planning to go talk to them about something."

"Maybe Joe and his friend are trying to get the Blackwells to do some sort of spy mission," suggested Benny.

"Or a private investigation," said Violet.

"Joe told us before that he's interested in the Blackwells' spider gate," Henry reminded them. "But there must be more to it than that, since we've seen both Joe and his friend watching the house."

"So what *is* going on?" Benny demanded.

"I don't know yet," said Jessie, "but I think we're close to figuring it out."

That night before bed, Henry peeked out his bedroom window. He was curious to see if Mr. Blackwell's light would be on again. The windows of the Blackwell house were dark, but Henry spotted something even stranger. Bright flashes of light were coming from the Blackwells' yard.

"What is that?" Henry said quietly to himself. The flashes were too bright to come from lightning bugs and too small to be real lightning. Henry thought they could have come from a strong flashlight, but why would someone be turning the flashlight on and off like that? Henry looked for flashes in the other neighbors' yards, but they only came from near the Blackwells' house.

Henry sat up, watching. Eventually the flashes stopped and Henry went back to bed.

The next morning over breakfast, Henry told the others what he'd seen. "Flashes?" asked Violet. "Like lightning?"

"Yes," said Henry. "But it wasn't lightning."

"If there had been a thunderstorm last night, I'd have known," said Benny. "I love thunder and lightning!"

"Come on, you guys," said Jessie. "I want to get to the museum to see what we can learn about spiders. Maybe we'll see something there that will help us figure out all these weird things that are going on."

"We should stop by and let Mrs. Blackwell know we won't be coming today," Violet said. "At least not until later."

The Aldens finished their cereal and put the bowls and spoons in the dishwasher. Then they got on their bikes. After they stopped at the Blackwells' house they were going to ride to the museum.

As they pedaled down the street, Benny said, "Not again!"

"What is it?" asked Violet

"That man is there again, Joe's friend. He's in front of the Blackwells' house," Benny said.

The others looked. Sure enough, the man was standing on the sidewalk facing the house, holding his hands up in front of his face. "What's he doing?" Henry wondered.

Jessie figured it out. "He's taking pictures! He's got a camera."

"You're right, Jessie!" said Violet. "Let's go talk to him to find out why."

Before they could reach him, the man tucked the camera into his jacket. He got into his car, which was parked at the curb. Then he sped off.

"You know, maybe that's what I saw last night," Henry said. "Maybe those flashes were from a camera!"

"You think that man was taking pictures in the Blackwells' yard at night?" Violet asked.

"I don't know," said Henry. "I don't know why he's taking pictures at all."

"I think we should tell the Blackwells," said Jessie. "I wouldn't want someone taking pictures of our house without our knowing. Who knows what he's up to."

"I agree," said Henry.

The children were turning into the Blackwells' driveway when Benny called, "Watch out!" A long, black limousine was coming down the driveway. The Aldens stopped just in time.

As the limo drove past, the children tried to see who was inside. There was a driver in front wearing a cap. But the back windows were tinted, making it impossible to see who, if anyone, was in the back.

The limo pulled out into the street, and the Aldens stood watching it for a moment.

"It's weird that the people inside can see us, but we can't see them," Violet said.

"I can't believe someone here in Greenfield drives around in a limo," said Jessie, "like a movie star."

"Or a top-secret spy," said Benny.

As usual, Mrs. Blackwell opened the door as soon as the children reached the front step.

"Hi," said Jessie. "Is it okay if we take the morning off today? We want to check out this spider exhibit we read about."

A strange look passed across Mrs. Blackwell's face.

"Would you like to go to the exhibit with us?" Henry asked.

"No," said Mrs. Blackwell, a little too quickly. Then she smiled. "That's fine — you've been working hard the last couple of days."

Henry looked thoughtful but said nothing.

"Mrs. Blackwell," said Jessie, "as we were walking here, we saw a man taking pictures of your house."

"You did?" Mrs. Blackwell said. She looked surprised.

"Yes, and we think he was here yesterday, with another man," Violet said.

"Oh, him," Mrs. Blackwell said. "He was taking pictures?"

"Yes," said Henry. "I think he might have been taking pictures last night, too. I saw some flashes of light in your backyard."

Mrs. Blackwell raised her eyebrows. "You don't miss anything, do you?"

Benny looked proud. "No, we don't. We like mysteries and we're good at finding clues. We haven't found a mystery yet we couldn't solve."

Mrs. Blackwell smiled, as if she had a secret. "I see," she said.

"So are you going to do something about the man taking pictures?" Jessie asked.

"Don't worry about him," said Mrs. Blackwell. "Have fun at the museum!"

"We'll come by tomorrow to see what

you need done," Henry offered, turning to go.

"Great," said Mrs. Blackwell. As the children stepped back outside, Mrs. Blackwell put her hand on the door to shut it behind them. As she lifted her arm, a thin gold bracelet slipped down her wrist and glinted in the sunlight. The bracelet held a single charm. Before she shut the door, the children caught a quick glimpse of the charm. It was a red hourglass.

CHAPTER 8

The Black Limousine

When the Aldens arrived at the museum, they were greeted by a large yellow banner hanging in front. Tall red letters on the banner spelled SPIDERS AND OTHER ARACHNIDS. Below the words was a picture of a giant spider.

"Here we are," said Henry. The Aldens parked their bikes and walked up the front steps.

Inside, the children asked the woman at the information desk where the spider exhibit was. "In there," she said, pointing to the main exhibit hall. The hall looked more crowded than the Aldens had ever seen it.

"This is the biggest exhibit we've had in a long time," the woman said.

"Really?" said Jessie.

"I had no idea it would be so popular," said the woman. "It just opened this morning and we've already had more people than some other exhibits draw in a whole week."

"I guess people are really interested in spiders," said Henry.

The Aldens entered the exhibit hall. Right in front of them was a model of a giant spider in a very realistic web.

"Wow!" said Benny.

"It's like something from a horror movie!" said Jessie.

"Of course!" said Henry, hitting his forehead with his palm. "A movie! *Beware the Spider's Bite!*"

The others looked at him strangely.

"Joe's jacket," Henry explained. "I knew it sounded familiar. Now I remember — *Beware the Spider's Bite* is a movie title. I saw posters for it last summer."

"I wonder why Joe has that jacket," said Violet.

"He must have really liked the movie," said Benny.

"I don't know," Henry said. "That jacket looked pretty special. I wonder if he actually worked on the movie — you know, helped to make it."

But Benny was no longer listening. He had just spotted something at the back of the exhibit hall. "Cool! There's a web back there you can climb on!" cried Benny, heading that way.

The others went off in different directions to see whatever interested them. Violet wanted to see the photographs of spiders that lined the walls. Jessie headed toward a diagram of a spider with labels identifying its different body parts. Next to the diagram there were models of spiderwebs and other kinds of spider traps. Henry studied some large maps showing which spiders came from which parts of the world.

When Benny reached the back of the hall, he quickly climbed onto the giant spi-

derweb made out of rope. Several other children were already climbing on it. Making his way to the top, Benny looked out at the room. He had a great view of the whole exhibit hall. It was crowded with visitors studying displays and museum staff helping them.

One person in the crowd caught Benny's eye. He was a short man with dark skin and shiny brown hair. He was wearing a long black coat. He stood off to one side of the exhibit hall, leaning against the wall. He looked right at Benny. When Benny's eyes met his, the man quickly turned and walked away.

The reason Benny noticed the man was that instead of looking at the exhibits like the other visitors, the man seemed to be studying the people in the crowd. As Benny watched, the man took a small notebook and a pen out of his jacket pocket. He jotted something down, then put the notebook quickly back into his pocket and strolled on.

Benny was fascinated. What was the man doing?

Benny looked around to see where his sisters and brother were. Henry and Violet were on the other side of the room, but Jessie was close by, studying the scorpion display.

Benny quickly climbed down the web. "Jessie," he called, hurrying over to her.

"Cool stuff, huh?" Jessie asked.

Benny nodded. "Yeah, but — "

"You'll never believe it — I touched a *tarantula* back there," Jessie said, pointing to the back of the hall. "It was really furry. I'm just glad I didn't have a spider like *that* on my back." She turned back to the scorpion photograph she'd been studying.

"Jessie, listen," Benny said.

Hearing the urgency in her brother's voice, Jessie turned away from the photo and looked at him. "What is it?"

Benny scanned the crowd until he spotted the man with the notebook. He was standing at the back of the hall.

Benny motioned with his head. "See that man back there?" he asked. "The one in the long black coat?"

Jessie looked. "Yes."

"Well, he's not looking at the exhibit — he's just watching the people," Benny said. "He was even watching me for a while."

"So?" Jessie asked.

"And he keeps writing in that little notebook," Benny added. "See?"

"Don't tell me you think he's a spy," said Jessie.

But Benny was too excited to notice that Jessie was teasing him. "Maybe he's working with Mrs. Blackwell." Then his eyes opened wider. "Or maybe he's the man she's trying to catch!"

Jessie sighed. "Wait a minute. Just because there have been some strange things happening on our street lately doesn't mean everyone in Greenfield is up to something." She strolled on to look at the next display.

But Benny was still focused on the mysterious man. He followed the man around the exhibit. The man definitely seemed to be studying the visitors more than the displays. Every now and then, he pulled out his notebook and made a quick note before tucking it back inside his coat. Benny tried to get a glimpse of what the man was writing, but he held the notebook too close to his chest.

"Hmmm . . ." said Benny. "Definitely up to something."

The man approached a door with an official-looking sign on it.

Benny looked at the sign on the door and sounded out the words. "St . . . staff . . . only. Staff only. Hey!" Benny said to himself, "he can't go in there!" The man wasn't wearing a museum uniform but he was headed straight for the door.

Benny stood facing the closed door, wondering what to do. Should he tell someone?

Before Benny could do anything, the man pulled the door open and went inside.

As the man shut the door behind him, Benny caught sight of something unexpected. On the man's wrist was a gold chain bracelet. The bracelet held a red hourglass charm.

Benny gasped. "I've got to find the others," he said to himself.

"Stop right there!" said a voice behind him.

Benny froze, startled. But when he turned around, he saw it was just Jessie, a big smile on her face.

"Jessie, you'll never believe it!" he said. "I was following that man and I saw something. He was wearing a bracelet!"

"So, some men wear jewelry," Jessie replied. "Benny, you've really got to stop — "

"But it had a red hourglass on it!" Benny said.

Jessie's eyes opened wide in surprise. "Really?" She frowned. "Let's go tell the others."

She and Benny found Henry and Violet in front of the giant spiderweb. Benny quickly told them about the mysterious man and the bracelet.

"How weird," said Violet.

"Come on," Henry said. "I want to see this guy. Let's try to find him."

As the Aldens headed around the room, Violet stopped in front of a photo of a spider wrapping a fly it had just caught in its web. "These photographs are amazing," she said.

"They are cool," said Jessie.

Then Violet smiled. "Hey, did you notice the name of the photographer? It says Arachnia Borrero. Mrs. Blackwell's name is Arachnia, too."

"That's funny," said Henry. "Arachnia can't be a very common name."

Benny looked away from the photograph toward the museum lobby. "Hey," he said. "There's the man!" He raced out of the exhibit.

The others chased Benny into the lobby after the mysterious man.

The man quickly crossed the lobby and headed out the front door of the museum. He was already down the steps and standing by the curb when the Aldens stepped out of the museum door.

A black limousine with dark-tinted windows pulled up to the curb. The Aldens watched as the back door opened and a white hand with shiny, red nails and a gold bracelet reached out. The hand grasped the man and seemed to pull him into the limousine. The car pulled away almost before the door was shut.

"That was Mrs. Blackwell!" said Benny. "She's caught the man she was looking for!"

CHAPTER 9

A Mystery Solved

Henry sat down on the front steps of the museum. This was going to take some figuring out. The others plopped down beside him.

"All right, what do we know about that man?" asked Jessie, pulling a pad of paper and a pen from her backpack.

"He was at the exhibit but he wasn't looking at the displays. He was just looking at the people," said Benny.

Jessie wrote that down. "And didn't you say he was writing in a notebook?" she asked.

"Yes," said Benny. "He also went in a door that's only supposed to be for museum staff."

Henry looked up when Benny said that. "Really?" he asked.

"Yes," said Benny. "The door said staff only."

"I think that may be the answer," said Henry. "I think that man must have worked on the exhibit."

"You do?" asked Benny. "Why?"

"That's why he went through that door," Henry explained. "That's why he wasn't interested in the exhibits, that's why he was watching the people. Remember this exhibit just opened. He was probably making sure things were running smoothly."

"That makes sense," said Jessie. "Maybe he's some kind of expert on spiders."

"He could be," said Henry.

"But what about his red hourglass bracelet that matches Mrs. Blackwell's?" Benny asked. "And the fact that he went off in her car?"

"That part makes sense to me," said Violet, who had been thinking quietly. "I bet he's her husband."

The children all looked at Violet.

"You think Mr. Blackwell is a spider expert?" asked Benny.

"Think about it," said Violet. "You saw a spider in a glass case in the room where he works. They've got a lot of books about spiders and maps labeled with their scientific names."

"He must have been working late at night to get this exhibit ready to open," Henry said, recalling the lights he saw in the middle of the night.

"And the bracelets?" asked Jessie.

"They're married," Violet said, "and they're both interested in spiders. What could be more romantic than wearing matching bracelets with a special symbol?"

"That would explain his unusual job," said Henry. "But what's hers?"

Benny frowned. "Secret agent," he said stubbornly.

"Well, we're not going to figure it out sitting here," Jessie pointed out. "Let's go back to their house."

The children unlocked their bikes and rode back to their street. They were almost at the Blackwells' house when they saw Joe and his friend standing on the sidewalk in front of the Blackwells' gate. The two men held a large piece of paper stretched between them. The children could make out some sort of diagram on the paper. Joe was pointing to the diagram and then pointing to the Blackwells' house. Deep in conversation, the two men didn't see the Aldens coming.

Henry motioned to the others to be quiet. He wanted to know what Joe was up to.

The children got off their bikes. They walked forward slowly, trying to catch what the men were talking about.

"This is the perfect place for it," Joe was saying. "We'll lay the trap right here and catch her in the web."

"Sounds good to me," said the other

man. "Let's just hope the Blackwells make the right choice."

Joe rolled up the diagram. The two men got in the car with the SPIDER2 license plate and drove off.

"Did you hear what they were saying?" asked Henry. "Setting a trap — catching someone in a web — the perfect place for it?"

"They're plotting to catch someone and it's going to happen here, in front of the Blackwells'," said Jessie.

"I'm worried," said Violet. "What if Mrs. Blackwell is the one they're planning to trap?"

The Aldens hurried up the driveway and parked their bikes. For the first time, they actually had to ring the bell before Mrs. Blackwell opened the door.

"Coming!" her voice called from within. A moment later she pulled the door open. "How was the exhibit?" she asked.

"Great!" said Henry, "but — "

"I'm in the middle of something," Mrs. Blackwell interrupted, a mysterious smile on her face. "You can go upstairs and start unpacking the boxes in the sitting room, if you'd like. I'll be up in a minute."

"Okay, but — " Henry began. He found himself talking to empty space. Mrs. Blackwell had already walked away. Henry turned to the others. "It will have to wait."

The Aldens went upstairs. The sitting room at the top of the stairs was filled with boxes labeled UPSTAIRS SITTING ROOM.

"This will keep us busy for a while," Jessie remarked, pulling over a box and ripping off the tape on top. The boxes were filled with books, framed pictures, and knickknacks. The Aldens got right to work.

Jessie had finished unpacking her first box when she noticed a box labeled SECOND FLOOR STORAGE. "That doesn't go in here," she said to herself. She picked up the box and looked around, trying to remember if Mrs. Blackwell had showed them a storage room.

She turned to the door with the lightbulb above it. The bulb was off now, so there was no red glow. "Maybe that room is a storage room or closet." Jessie walked over and slowly pushed open the door. Immediately she knew this was not an ordinary closet. This room was very dark and she could smell a strong chemical odor.

Jessie was so surprised, she didn't stop to think. She took a step into the room. It was larger than a closet but there seemed to be no windows. Jessie put the box down and felt on the wall for a light switch. There were two. When she flicked on the first, nothing happened inside the room, but Jessie noticed a red glow behind her. Poking her head back out, Jessie saw that the lightbulb over the door was on, as it had been that day she'd come upstairs.

Jessie remembered her idea that maybe the light was a warning not to go in the mysterious room. But why?

She flicked the other switch, and the lights inside the room came on. On the far wall was a counter holding several flat trays of fluid. Shelves underneath were filled with large bottles of chemicals. Strung up above was a sort of clothesline. But there was no clothing on this line. Instead there were long curls of film and photographs held up by clothespins.

Unable to contain her curiosity, Jessie stepped forward. She peered at one of the photographs. It showed a large spiderweb with a brownish spider in the center. The next photograph was also of a spider, but this one was yellow and black, like the one that had been on her back. She looked at the next photograph. It was a spider, too, and so was the next, and the next, and the next. All the photos were of spiders, different sizes and colors, taken from different angles. They were beautiful, just like the ones on display at the museum.

Jessie's mind raced back to the exhibit. The name below the photos had been Arachnia Borrero. Mrs. Blackwell's first name was Arachnia. As Henry had pointed out, Arachnia was an unusual name for two people to share. Maybe there weren't two different people, Jessie realized. Maybe there was just one Arachnia using two different last names.

"She's a photographer," Jessie said to herself. She took one more look at all the photos.

Jessie turned around and gasped in surprise. Standing right behind her was Mrs. Blackwell. Violet, Henry, and Benny were beside her.

"You're a photographer, aren't you?" asked Jessie. "You took the photos for the exhibit!"

Something in Mrs. Blackwell's stiff posture and face seemed to soften, as if she were relaxing for the first time. A smile spread slowly across her face. "Yes. Those are my photos."

"They're beautiful," said Violet. "Your work is amazing."

"But the pictures at the exhibit were taken by Arachnia Borrero," said Henry, confused.

Mrs. Blackwell nodded. "That's me."

Benny grinned. "A secret code name?"

Mrs. Blackwell's smile grew. "You have a wonderful imagination, Benny. Not a code name, just my maiden name. Before I married I was Borrero, and I still use that name for my work."

"Why didn't you tell us that you're a photographer?" asked Violet.

"Well," said Mrs. Blackwell, "I have to be careful. Some people just don't understand."

"That you're a photographer?" asked Violet. "But what a wonderful job!"

"Oh, that's not the part they have a problem with," Mrs. Blackwell said. "It's *what* I choose to photograph that causes problems." She smiled at the children's puzzled faces.

"When I tell people I'm a photographer, they ask if I do weddings or sunsets or portraits of children," Mrs. Blackwell explained. "When I tell them I only photograph spiders, people get upset. They think I should only take pictures of 'beautiful things.' Well, to me, spiders are beautiful. Some people think that makes me . . . strange."

"I think it's pretty cool," said Jessie.

"Yeah," agreed Henry and Violet.

Mrs. Blackwell looked at Benny, who'd

been silently looking at the floor. "What's the matter, Benny? You look disappointed."

"Spider pictures are okay," Benny said. "But I was hoping you were a spy."

Mrs. Blackwell looked surprised. "A *spy*?" she repeated. "Why would you think I was a spy?"

"Because you said on the phone you were tracking someone down but you hadn't caught them yet and time was running out," Benny said.

Mrs. Blackwell began to laugh, something the Aldens had never seen her do before.

"Were you talking about a spider?" asked Violet. "A special one you wanted to photograph?"

Mrs. Blackwell nodded, still laughing. "You must have heard me talking to my editor. I've been trying to photograph a very rare type of spider for a new book and I've had a hard time tracking it down. They want to print the book, so they've been pressuring me to get the photo."

"And you don't want the spider to know

you're there," said Violet. "To catch it in the act of spinning its web."

"This kind of spider hides if it senses people are around," Mrs. Blackwell explained.

"Do you photograph spiders all around the world?" Jessie asked. "And mark their locations in your atlas?"

"So you saw my atlas," Mrs. Blackwell said, nodding.

"And to travel around the world you need to know different languages," Violet said, figuring out the reason for the dictionaries. Suddenly everything was beginning to make sense.

"That diagram in the library . . . did it show the location of a special spider?" Jessie asked. Mrs. Blackwell frowned for a moment, not sure what Jessie was talking about. "The paper on the desk," Jessie said.

"Oh!" Mrs. Blackwell said. "You really are detectives. I spotted an unusual web out beyond the tall grass. I drew a diagram so I could go back and check it out later."

"And you did go back!" said Henry. "Last

night, to take pictures. Those were the flashes I saw from my bedroom window."

"But what about all those books about spies?" asked Benny, not wanting to let go of the idea that Mrs. Blackwell was a secret agent.

"Oh, they're just for fun — I love to read spy thrillers," Mrs. Blackwell said. "My sister Amy is a mystery writer, and I collect all her books." She chuckled. "Me, a spy. Wait until my husband hears that."

"We saw your husband at the museum!" Benny said. "At least we think it was him."

"You hadn't met him before? He's been so busy . . . Wait here a minute." Mrs. Blackwell left the room and reappeared a moment later. "Let me introduce my husband." She turned around as a man several inches shorter than Mrs. Blackwell came in behind her. He was the man from the museum.

"You're a spider expert, right?" asked Henry. "You study spiders in that room at the back of the house."

"That is right," Mr. Blackwell said. "I am a scientist, and that is my laboratory. I'm sorry that I haven't had the chance to say hello before this but I don't like to be disturbed when I'm working — and I have been working very hard."

"Do you work with black widow spiders?" Jessie asked.

"Yes," he said. "Others as well, but those are my specialty."

"That's why your boxes have red hourglasses on them," Jessie said. "And why you two wear those bracelets."

Mrs. Blackwell and her husband smiled at each other. "We met while working on an article about black widows," Mrs. Blackwell explained. "When we got married, we got these matching bracelets. It's our little symbol. And, yes, we put it on the boxes that contained my husband's delicate equipment."

"We really enjoyed the museum exhibit," said Henry. "We learned a lot!"

Mr. Blackwell sighed and looked at his

wife, who smiled back. "Thank you. This is the biggest exhibit of my career and I want it to do well." Mr. Blackwell said. "If it does, I may get a permanent job at the museum."

"I think you're going to get that job," said Violet. "The woman at the front desk said they had a bigger crowd there today than they've had in a long time."

The Blackwells smiled.

"I still don't understand why you tried to hide what your jobs are," said Jessie. "Why didn't you tell us?"

Mr. and Mrs. Blackwell looked at each other. Then he spoke. "We have had problems with our neighbors in the past. One neighbor became afraid when he learned I had a laboratory in the house where I studied poisonous spiders. The neighbor did not understand that I am very careful. We make sure our house is safe." Mr. Blackwell looked at his wife grimly. "Our former neighbors made things so difficult for us, we had to move." He sighed. "This time we decided we would do as the spiders do and hide ourselves away."

"That's why you built those big walls in front," Jessie said.

"Exactly," said Mrs. Blackwell.

"And do you have secret cameras to see who's coming?" asked Benny.

The Blackwells looked at each other, confused. "Secret cameras?"

"You always saw us coming before we rang the bell," Jessie said.

Mrs. Blackwell smiled and motioned to a desk that was in front of a window. "That's my desk," she said. "I often sit there to work. Go look."

The children went over to the desk. From the window they could see the front walk clearly. They smiled sheepishly and turned away from the window.

"You see," Mrs. Blackwell said. "No secret cameras."

Suddenly, Benny frowned. "There's one part of this mystery I still don't get," he said, crossing his arms.

"What part is that?" asked Mr. Blackwell.

"Part two," said Benny. "Joe Toll."

"Part two . . ." echoed Violet, her face lighting up with excitement. "Benny, that's it!"

CHAPTER 10

Movie Stars

Henry, Jessie, and Benny stared blankly at Violet. "That's *what*?" Benny asked.

"That's the answer — that's what Joe Toll and his friend are doing," Violet explained.

"You've lost us, Violet," Henry said. "Go back to the beginning."

"Remember how you figured out that Joe might have a connection to that movie, *Beware the Spider's Bite*?" Violet said.

Henry nodded.

"Well, I think you're right," Violet continued. "I think Joe Toll made that movie.

And I think he's planning to make another one — *Spider Two*, like it says on the license plate."

"That makes sense," Jessie said. "But why have they been hanging around the Blackwells' house?"

"They haven't," said Violet. "They've been hanging around the Blackwells' *gate*. My guess is that they want to use the gate in their spider movie — that they want to film a scene here." Violet looked at Mr. and Mrs. Blackwell. The Blackwells looked impressed.

Before Violet could continue, Benny jumped in. "So when Joe was talking about setting a trap and catching someone in a web, he was describing what will happen in the movie," he said.

Henry looked at the Blackwells. "But you don't want them to film here," he guessed. "You told Joe and his friend you weren't interested."

The Blackwells looked at each other. Henry couldn't read their expressions. Mr. Blackwell turned back to the Aldens.

"We told them we would think about it," he said, "that we'll consider their offer. But — "

Just then, the doorbell rang. Mrs. Blackwell lifted an eyebrow. "That's probably them now," she said. She walked downstairs to open the door. The Aldens and Mr. Blackwell followed.

Sure enough, there were Joe Toll and his friend standing on the doorstep. Joe was carrying a briefcase and a large piece of posterboard. Both men were wearing *Beware the Spider's Bite* jackets.

"Come in," Mrs. Blackwell said, leading them into the living room. "Please sit down." She motioned for the children to join them also. "I understand you have already met the Aldens," she said.

"Well, hello," Joe said to the children. "Nice to see you again. This is my brother Vince."

Vince nodded hello.

"We've seen you before," Benny said to Vince, "when you were checking out the Blackwells' gate."

Vince smiled. "That gate is exactly what we're here to talk about," he said.

"When Vince drove by and saw that spider gate, he told me this was the perfect place to film our next movie," said Joe. "I agree. We'd like to film *Beware the Spider's Bite II* right here in Greenfield — and the most important scene in the movie would take place in front of that gate."

"So that's why you asked us all those questions about the neighborhood," Jessie guessed. "You were trying to find out if this would be a good place to film, weren't you?"

Joe nodded. "We want to film in a friendly neighborhood. It's more pleasant to work someplace when the people who live there are nice about having you around."

"It would be exciting to have a movie filmed on our street," said Henry, glancing at the Blackwells.

"I've brought a diagram to show how great the gates would look at the climax of the movie," Joe said hurriedly, before the Blackwells could reply. He held up the posterboard, which was adorned with photos of the front of the house.

"We saw Vince taking those pictures," said Violet.

"You see, we'd zoom in on the spider design," Joe continued. "The bad guys would have a trap set up right there."

"Wow!" said Benny. "That would be exciting!"

"I think it would be," Joe agreed. "But it all depends on the Blackwells." He turned to Mr. and Mrs. Blackwell. "You don't look convinced."

"I am a scientist," said Mr. Blackwell. "I deal in facts, not fantasy. I don't appreciate the way movies can make innocent spiders look like monsters."

Joe nodded. "As we discussed before, the movie is a thriller, so we want it to be exciting. But we're hoping you can help us make it as accurate as possible."

"Give me a copy of the script," said Mrs. Blackwell. "If my husband and I like it, we'll consider letting you film here."

"Great!" said Joe. He opened his briefcase and pulled out a bound set of papers, which he handed to Mrs. Blackwell.

When Joe and Vince had left, Mrs. Blackwell turned to the others. "Imagine, our home in a movie. That would be kind of thrilling! Well . . . I think it's time for some refreshments." Mrs. Blackwell went into the kitchen and came out a moment later with a plate of cupcakes, which she set down on the coffee table.

"Look at those!" cried Benny. The cupcakes were iced with white frosting and swirling black spiderwebs.

"For my wonderful helpers," said Mrs. Blackwell. "I was just taking these out of the oven when you arrived."

"So that's why you walked away so quickly," said Henry.

"I didn't want them to burn," Mrs. Blackwell said.

Everyone took a cupcake.

"I'm glad all of the mysteries have been explained," said Violet.

"I'm not," said Benny.

"No?" asked Mrs. Blackwell.

"No," said Benny. "I would have been much happier if you'd been a spy."

The next night, when the Aldens set the table for dinner, they added two extra places at the end. Benny had just set down the last spoon and Violet had just finished arranging the flowers on the table when the doorbell rang. Watch barked and ran to the door, his tail wagging.

Grandfather opened the door. His grandchildren gathered eagerly behind him. "Nice to see you again, Mrs. Blackwell," said Mr. Alden, putting out a hand to shake hers. "And you must be Mr. Blackwell. Please come in. My grandchildren have told me all about you."

"They are wonderful kids," said Mrs. Blackwell. "And a tremendous help to me and my husband."

"I am very fortunate to have such nice grandchildren," said Mr. Alden, leading the Blackwells into the living room. They sat in two chairs beside the fireplace, while the Aldens settled on the sofas.

"It is nice of you to have us over for dinner," said Mrs. Blackwell. "Our neighbors have not always been so welcoming."

"I'm sorry to hear that," said Mr. Alden.

"But that is past," said Mr. Blackwell. "We have some news. We have read the script for *Beware the Spider's Bite II.*"

"And?" Benny asked excitedly, moving to the edge of his seat.

"And I told them we would agree to let them film it in front of our house — on one condition." Mrs. Blackwell paused. "We said they must use four local children in the movie as extras."

"Four children," Benny repeated. "Do you mean . . . ?"

Mrs. Blackwell nodded. "I mean my favorite detectives — and neighbors. The Alden children."

"And what did they say?" Jessie wanted to know.

Mrs. Blackwell took her time before answering, a smile spreading across her face. "What could they say? They said yes, of course."

"We're going to be in the movie?" Violet asked, unable to believe it.

The Blackwells nodded.

"Hooray!" cried Benny. "It's not quite as good as having spies on our street — but almost!"

Scary Spiders!

Black widow spiders? Yikes! The Aldens are caught up in a very creepy mystery. Henry, Jessie, Violet, and Benny will have to keep their wits about them to untangle the latest clues.

How about you? Would you know an arachnid from an anteater? Test your detective skills with the following spidery activities. Grab a pencil and have fun. And remember, be nice to our eight-legged friends!

Spiderweb Maze

The fly is trying to escape the sticky spiderweb. Can you help her find her way through the maze to freedom?

Creepy Crawly Copies

If the six spiders below seem identical at first glance, just look a little closer. One of these spiders is different from the rest. Can you circle the spider that's unique?

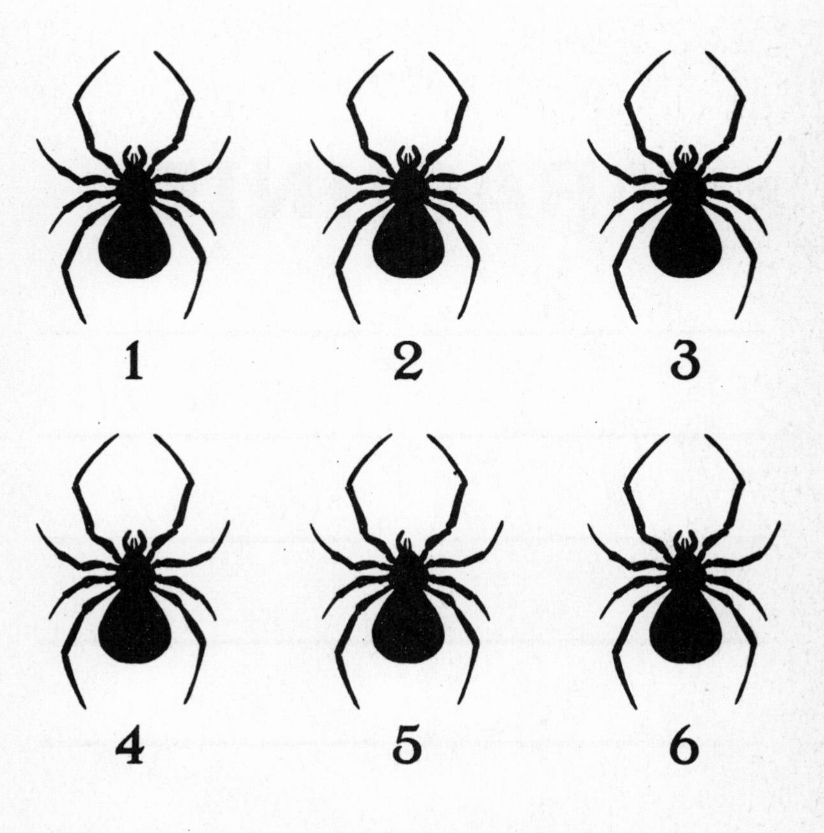

Spider Spell-Off

Scientists call eight-legged creatures like spiders *arachnids*. It's a fun word to say — and even more fun to play around with. Using only the letters found in arachnid, how many other words can you spell? (For example, using the *r*, the *a*, the *c*, and the *d*, you can spell *card*.) Write the new words in the spaces below.

ARACHNID

________________ ________________

________________ ________________

________________ ________________

________________ ________________

________________ ________________

Make-a-Web

Spiders spin complex webs in which they live, eat, and sleep. If you were a spider, what would your web look like? Draw it in the space below. You could even draw yourself, in spider form, on it!

Sneaky Spiders!

When they don't want to be found, spiders are great at hiding. Can you find and circle all ten spiders hidden in this library?

Spider Scramble

The names of some common spiders are scrambled below. Can you solve each scramble and write the names of the spiders correctly on the lines provided?

1. CLBAK IWWOD ____________________
2. ADDYD NOLG SGLE ____________________
3. ATRAUTLAN ____________________
4. RWBON CRLSUEE ____________________
5. PMUNIJG ____________________

The Spider Scene

Good detectives must be very observant. Test your skills by carefully studying the picture below for one full minute. Then try to answer the questions on the next page — without peeking! Ready? Go!

Questions:

1. How many spiders are in the web?

   ____

2. How many birds are outside the window?

   ____

3. Is it daytime or nighttime?

   ____

4. Are there curtains on the window?

   ____

5. How many books are on the windowsill?

   ____

6. In which corner of the window have the spiders built their web?

   ____

Tangled Webs

These spiders are all mixed up! Can you help each spider find the way back to her web? Hurry—dinner is waiting!

Spider Surprise

What's hidden in the spider's web? Connect the dots to find out!

Benny's Joke

Benny made up a joke inspired by the Aldens' spider mystery adventure. Circle the capital letters you see below and put them together to find the punch line.

What's a spider's favorite day of the week?

k r W n E l e B u q t N v s E h g p S D h v A d e Y w

Answer: __ __ __ __ __ __ __ __ __ !

Answers

Spiderweb Maze

Creepy Crawly Copies

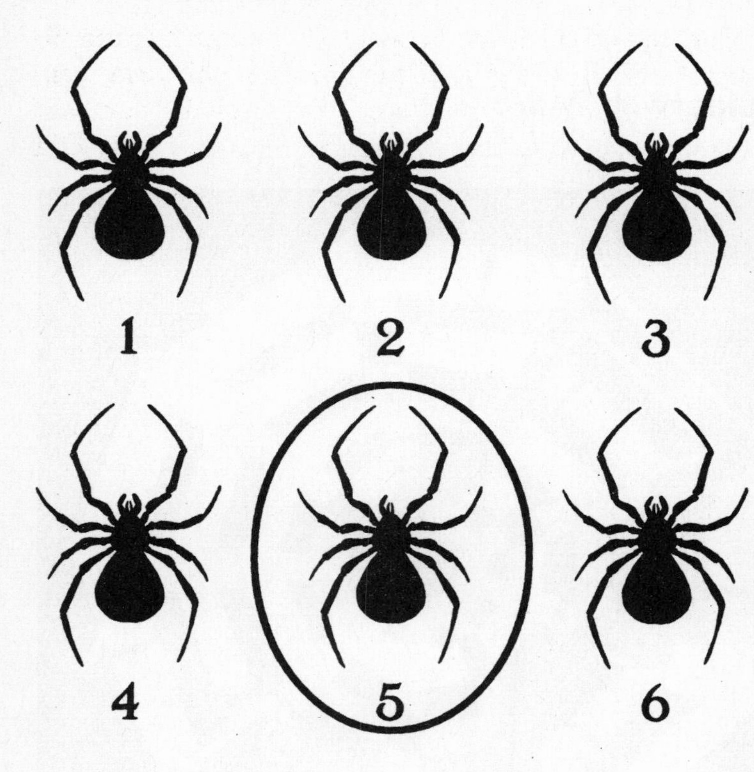

Spider Spell-Off

You can make a lot of words out of the letters in ARACHNID! We spelled: din, hid, chin, rid, can, ran, and, hand, hind, hard, drain, chair, hair, air, raid, rain, arc, arch, car, card, had, darn, chain. Did you find any others?

Sneaky Spiders!

Spider Scramble

1. Black Widow
2. Daddy Long Legs
3. Tarantula
4. Brown Recluse
5. Jumping

The Spider Scene

1. Two
2. One
3. Daytime
4. No, there are shutters
5. Three
6. The upper left hand corner

Tangled Webs

Spider Surprise

Benny's Joke

What's a spider's favorite day of the week?

*Web*nesday!

GERTRUDE CHANDLER WARNER discovered when she was teaching that many readers who like an exciting story could find no books that were both easy and fun to read. She decided to try to meet this need, and her first book, *The Boxcar Children*, quickly proved she had succeeded.

Miss Warner drew on her own experiences to write the mystery. As a child she spent hours watching trains go by on the tracks opposite her family home. She often dreamed about what it would be like to set up housekeeping in a caboose or freight car — the situation the Alden children find themselves in.

When Miss Warner received requests for more adventures involving Henry, Jessie, Violet, and Benny Alden, she began additional stories. In each, she chose a special setting and introduced unusual or eccentric characters who liked the unpredictable.

While the mystery element is central to each of Miss Warner's books, she never thought of them as strictly juvenile mysteries. She liked to stress the Aldens' independence and resourcefulness and their solid New England devotion to using up and making do. The Aldens go about most of their adventures with as little adult supervision as possible — something else that delights young readers.

Miss Warner lived in Putnam, Connecticut, until her death in 1979. During her lifetime, she received hundreds of letters from girls and boys telling her how much they liked her books.